The Touchstone

A Fable by
Robert Louis Stevenson
Pictures by
Uri Shulevitz

 Greenwillow Books
A Division of William Morrow & Company, Inc., New York

To Ezekiel Shtreichman,
my first painting teacher

1 2 3 4 5 80 79 78 77 76

Library of Congress Cataloging in Publication Data
Stevenson, Robert Louis, 1850-1894. The touchstone.
Summary: Two princes desirous of marrying the same princess are
told that whoever shall find the touchstone of truth shall win her.
[1. Fairy tales] I. Shulevitz, Uri (date) II. Title. PZ8.S617T03
[E] 76-3412 ISBN 0-688-80051-3 ISBN 0-688-84051-5 lib. bdg.

I am grateful to Dr. Isabel Wright for introducing me to *The Touchstone*, a story which she has found useful and evocative in her psychiatric practice and her private life, and which, as an artist, I have found equally stimulating and enlightening.

Uri Shulevitz

The gift of truth is beautiful and precious. The truth may bring a joyful or a sad message, but it is strong as the heart and aware as the mind, and no less than the most of both.

In this fable the elder son goes in search of the touchstone of truth that is to win him a beautiful princess and a kingdom for a home. On his return with the true touchstone he finds that the prize is gone. His brother has married the princess and owns the kingdom. First he weeps, then he turns on them the touchstone and sees that they have no prize at all in each other and that their way of living, which is less than the total human potential, is too high a price to pay for a kingdom. In the light of the true touchstone he sees them as they are and as they were really all the time. And in this seeing, he is freed to know the truth and the world in all their variety and interest, not to know only the dull, repetitive and partial images of the truth and the world as reflected in the many false touchstones he was given by others on his journey. "How if this be the truth? that all are a little true?" the elder son exclaims, when he sees that each one of these partial touchstones has some beauty in the light of the true touchstone, while in one another's light they are as dull as coal. He sees that partial truths contradict one another and show one another to be dull and hateful, while the true touchstone, in showing the comprehensive reality that is always around us and with us, reveals what is good, as well as what is bad, in each partial truth.

The Touchstone might be called a moral allegory. Robert Louis Stevenson wrote this and other fables during the last seven years of his life, which ended in 1894 at the age of forty-four.

Isabel Wright, M.D.

THE King was a man that stood well before the world, his smile was sweet as clover, but his soul withinsides was as little as a pea. He had two sons; and the younger son was a boy after his heart, but the elder was one whom he feared.

It befell one morning that the drum sounded in the dun before it was yet day; and the King rode with his two sons, and a brave array behind them. They rode two hours, and came to the foot of a brown mountain that was very steep.

"Where do we ride?" said the elder son.

"Across this brown mountain," said the King, and smiled to himself.

"My father knows what he is doing," said the younger son.

And they rode two hours more, and came to the sides of a black river that was wondrous deep.

"And where do we ride?" asked the elder son.

"Over this black river," said the King, and smiled to himself.

"My father knows what he is doing," said the younger son.

And they rode all that day, and about the time of the sunsetting came to the side of a lake, where was a great dun.

"It is here we ride," said the King; "to a King's house, and a priest's, and a house where you will learn much."

At the gates of the dun, the King who was a priest met them, and he was a grave man, and beside him stood his daughter, and she was as fair as the morn, and one that smiled and looked down.

"These are my two sons," said the first King.

"And here is my daughter," said the King who was a priest.

"She is a wonderful fine maid," said the first King, "and I like her manner of smiling."

"They are wonderful well-grown lads," said the second, "and I like their gravity."

And then the two Kings looked at each other, and said, "The thing may come about."

And in the meanwhile the two lads looked upon the maid, and the one grew pale and the other red; and the maid looked upon the ground smiling.

"Here is the maid that I shall marry," said the elder. "For I think she smiled upon me."

But the younger plucked his father by the sleeve. "Father," said he, "a word in your ear. If I find favor in your sight, might not I wed this maid, for I think she smiles upon me?"

"A word in yours," said the King his father. "Waiting is good hunting, and when the teeth are shut the tongue is at home."

Before it was day, the elder son arose, and he found the maid at her weaving, for she was a diligent girl. "Maid," quoth he, "I would fain marry you."

"You must speak with my father," said she, and she looked upon the ground smiling, and became like the rose.

"Her heart is with me," said the elder son, and he went down to the lake and sang.

A little after came the younger son. "Maid," quoth he, "if our fathers were agreed, I would like well to marry you."

"You can speak to my father," said she, and looked upon the ground and smiled and grew like the rose.

"She is a dutiful daughter," said the younger son, "she will make an obedient wife." And then he thought, "What shall I do?" and he remembered the King her father was a priest; so he went into the temple and sacrificed a weasel and a hare.

Presently the news got about; and the two lads and the first King were called into the presence of the King who was a priest, where he sat upon the high seat.

"Little I reck of gear," said the King who was a priest, "and little of power. For we live here among the shadows of things, and the heart is sick of seeing them. And we stay here in the wind like raiment drying, and the heart is weary of the wind. But one thing I love, and that is truth; and for one thing will I give my daughter, and that is the trial stone. For in the light of that stone the seeming goes, and the being shows, and all things besides are worthless. Therefore, lads, if ye would wed my daughter, out foot, and bring me the stone of touch, for that is the price of her."

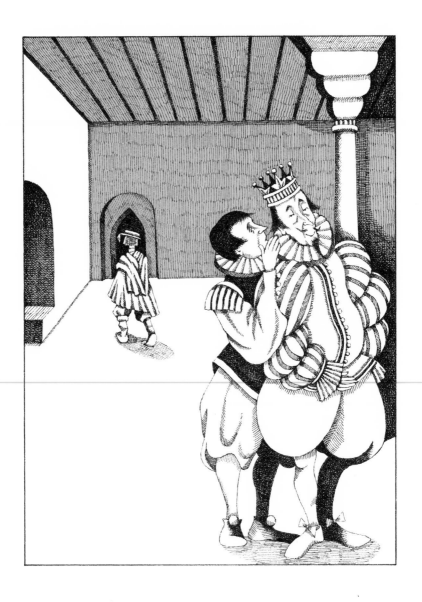

"A word in your ear," said the younger son to his father. "I think we do very well without this stone."

"A word in yours," said his father. "I am of your way of thinking; but when the teeth are shut the tongue is at home." And he smiled to the King that was a priest.

But the elder son got to his feet, and called the King that was a priest by the name of father. "For whether I marry the maid or no, I will call you by that word for the love of your wisdom; and even now I will ride forth and search the world for the stone of touch." So he said farewell and rode into the world.

"I think I will go, too," said the younger son, "if I can have your leave. For my heart goes out to the maid."

"You will ride home with me," said his father.

So they rode home, and when they came to the dun, the King had his son into his treasury. "Here," said he, "is the touchstone which shows truth; for there is no truth but plain truth; and if you will look in this, you will see yourself as you are."

And the younger son looked in it, and saw his face as it were the face of a beardless youth, and he was well enough pleased; for the thing was a piece of a mirror.

"Here is no such great thing to make a work about," said he; "but if it will get me the maid, I shall never complain. But what a fool is my brother to ride into the world, and the thing all the while at home."

So they rode back to the other dun, and showed the mirror to the King that was a priest; and when he had looked in it, and seen himself like a King, and his house like a King's house, and all things like themselves, he cried out and blessed God. "For now I know," said he, "there is no truth but the plain truth; and I am a King indeed, although my heart misgave me." And he pulled down his temple, and built a new one; and then the younger son was married to the maid.

In the meantime the elder son rode into the world to find the touchstone of the trial of truth; and whenever he came to a place of habitation, he would ask the men if they had heard of it. And in every place the men answered: "Not only have we heard of it, but we, alone of all men, possess the thing itself, and it hangs in the side of our chimney to this day." Then would the elder son be glad, and beg for a sight of it. And sometimes it would be a piece of mirror, that showed the seeming of things, and then he would say, "This can never be, for there should be more than seeming." And sometimes it would be a lump of coal, which showed nothing; and then he would say, "This can never be, for at least there is the seeming."

And sometimes it would be a touchstone indeed, beautiful in hue, adorned with polishing, the light inhabiting its sides; and when he found this, he would beg the thing, and the persons of that place would give it him, for all men were very generous of that gift; so that at the last he had his wallet full of them, and they chinked together when he rode; and when he halted by the side of the way he would take them out and try them, till his head turned like the sails upon a windmill.

Now after many years the elder son came upon the sides of the salt sea; and it was night, and a savage place, and the clamor of the sea was loud. There he was aware of a house, and a man that sat there by the light of a candle, for he had no fire. Now the elder son came in to him, and the man gave him water to drink, for he had no bread; and wagged his head when he was spoken to, for he had no words.

"Have you the touchstone of truth?" asked the elder son; and when the man had wagged his head, "I might have known that," cried the elder son, "I have here a wallet full of them!" And with that he laughed, although his heart was weary.

And with that the man laughed too, and with the fuff of his laughter the candle went out.

"Sleep," said the man, "for now I think you have come far enough; and your quest is ended, and my candle is out."

Now when the morning came, the man gave him a clear pebble in his hand, and it had no beauty and no color, and the elder son looked upon it scornfully and shook his head, and he went away, for it seemed a small affair to him.

All that day he rode, and his mind was quiet, and the desire of the chase allayed. "How if this poor pebble be the touchstone, after all?" said he; and he got down from his horse, and emptied forth his wallet by the side of the way.

Now, in the light of each other, all the touchstones lost their hue and fire and withered like stars at morning; but in the light of the pebble their beauty remained, only the pebble was the most bright. And the elder son smote upon his brow. "How if this be the truth?" he cried, "that all are a little true?" And he took the pebble, and turned its light upon the heavens, and they deepened above him like the pit; and he turned it on the hills, and the hills were cold and rugged, but life ran in their sides so that his own life bounded; and he turned it on the dust, and he beheld the dust with joy and terror; and he turned it on himself, and kneeled down and prayed.

"Now thanks be to God," said the elder son, "I have found the touchstone; and now I may turn my reins, and ride home to the King and to the maid of the dun that makes my mouth to sing and my heart enlarge."

Now when he came to the dun, he saw children playing by the gate where the King had met him in the old days; and this stayed his pleasure, for he thought in his heart, "It is here my children should be playing." And when he came into the hall, there was his brother on the high seat and the maid beside him; and at that his anger rose, for he thought in his heart, "It is I that should be sitting there, and the maid beside me."

"Who are you?" said his brother. "And what make you in the dun?"

"I am your elder brother," he replied. "And I am come to marry the maid, for I have brought the touchstone of truth."

Then the younger brother laughed aloud. "Why," said he, "I found the touchstone years ago, and married the maid, and there are our children playing at the gate."

Now at this the elder brother grew as gray as the dawn. "I pray you have dealt justly," said he, "for I perceive my life is lost."

"Justly?" quoth the younger brother. "It becomes you ill, that are a restless man and a runagate, to doubt my justice or the King my father's that are sedentary folk and known in the land."

"Nay," said the elder brother, "you have all else, have patience also; and suffer me to say the world is full of touchstones, and it appears not easily which is true."

"I have no shame of mine," said the younger brother. "There it is, and look in it."

So the elder brother looked in the mirror, and he was sore amazed; for he was an old man, and his hair was white upon his head; and he sat down in the hall and wept aloud.

"Now," said the younger brother, "see what a fool's part you have played, that ran over all the world to seek what was lying in our father's treasury, and came back an old carle for the dogs to bark at, and without chick or child. And I that was dutiful and wise sit here crowned with virtues and pleasures, and happy in the light of my hearth."

"Methinks you have a cruel tongue," said the elder brother; and he pulled out the clear pebble and turned its light on his brother; and behold the man was lying, his soul was shrunk into the smallness of a pea, and his heart was a bag of little fears like scorpions, and love was dead in his bosom. And at that the elder brother cried out aloud, and turned the light of the pebble on the maid, and lo! she was but a mask of a woman, and withinsides she was quite dead, and she smiled as a clock ticks and knew not wherefore.

"Oh, well," said the elder brother, "I perceive there is both good and bad. So fare ye all as well as ye may in the dun; but I will go forth into the world with my pebble in my pocket."